Some Swahili Words

Afua
to save, pardon, cure

Beba
to carry, transport

Joka
big snake

Pumbaa
to be stunned, at a loss for words

Simba
lion

Disney's

THE
LION KING

SNAKE IN THE GRASS

by Leslie McGuire

Illustrations by Laureen Burger
Brooks & Rachelle Campbell
Denise Shimabukuro

Produced by Mega-Books, Inc. Design and art direction by Michaelis/Carpelis Design Assoc., Inc.
Printed in the United States of America.

Grolier Books

ISBN: 0-7172-8351-8

CHAPTER 1

H ey, Pumbaa!" cried Timon, sitting straight up on a log. "Why are most leaves green?"

"Er, uh, I'm not sure," said Pumbaa. He shook his head and grunted. The sun was getting hot, but it was shady under the acacia tree.

Timon, a meerkat, and Pumbaa, his warthog friend, were getting ready for their early-afternoon nap. It was halfway between their after-lunch nap and their late-afternoon nap.

"Leaves are green," said Timon, "because that big yellow thing in the sky puts special green glop on them."

"Wow," said Pumbaa. "That's amazing. I kind of thought it was because the green stuff helps them make food from light."

"Boy, don't you know anything?" said Timon. "That's crazy! Making food from light! Hah!"

"Can I go back to sleep now?" asked Pumbaa.

"Yeah, sure," said Timon. "I just thought maybe you'd like to talk about science or—"

Thump! Crash!

"Oof!" Pumbaa grunted.

The lion cub Kopa had raced through the bushes, jumped over the log, and run smack into Pumbaa's stomach. Nala, Kopa's mother, was right behind him.

"Whoa, whoa, whoa, little buddy," said Timon, hopping on top of Pumbaa.

Nala laughed. "Kopa, you're just like Simba when he was your age."

Simba, the Lion King, was Kopa's father. Nala and Simba had known each other ever since they were cubs. When Simba's father, Mufasa, had been killed, Simba had run away because he'd thought his father's death was his fault. But Mufasa had been killed by his evil brother, Scar, who wanted to be the Lion King.

Timon and Pumbaa had rescued Simba, and they had lived in a jungle far away until Nala had found Simba. Nala had persuaded Simba to take his rightful place as king. Simba had battled Scar and become the new Lion King. Not long after, Nala and Simba had become the parents of Kopa.

Kopa crinkled his nose and sniffed loudly.

"What's bothering you?" asked Nala gently. "Something is wrong."

"Nothing," Kopa said, turning his head away and sniffing again.

"Something's wrong?" asked Timon, hopping down from Pumbaa's back and onto a rock. "What happened?"

"Nothing happened!" Kopa yelled. "And stop asking me all the time!"

"See?" said Nala. "He's grouchy. Something's wrong, but Kopa keeps saying everything is fine. I don't believe him!"

"I'm sure everything is okay," Timon said to Nala. He patted Kopa on the head. "Leave Kopa here with us. I think he just needs to talk about science for awhile."

"Science always cheers me up!" Pumbaa grunted. "I love science!"

Nala turned to Kopa. "Have a good time," she said. She walked away from the acacia tree and headed back across the grassy plain to Pride Rock.

"Just leave it to old Uncle Timon and old Uncle Pumbaa," said Timon, punching Kopa's shoulder. "Sometimes a man needs to talk about stuff with another man, right?"

Kopa rolled his eyes and clamped his mouth shut. He looked disgusted.

Timon sat down facing Kopa. "So what's the problem?" he asked. "You can tell us. Is it a girl or something?"

"Did one of the girl cubs knock you down?" asked Pumbaa. "Your mother always used to knock your father down when they were cubs. Simba got really mad about that."

Kopa looked up, surprised.

"She did?" he said. "I didn't think anyone could knock Dad down."

"Not now," said Timon. "But back then, it was a different story. Is that what happened?"

"No!" said Kopa. "And I don't feel like talking about it. That's all."

"Boy, oh, boy," mumbled Timon. "Our little buddy is not in a good mood."

"Well, sometimes talking about a problem helps," said Pumbaa.

"Just leave me alone!" snapped Kopa. He turned his head and stared at some springbok bouncing across the plain.

A tear rolled down Kopa's face. He sniffed hard and scowled. "Who cares anyway?"

"Not me," said Timon. He folded his arms across his chest. "I only care about grubs and bugs. How about you, Pumbaa? What do you care about?"

"Gosh," said Pumbaa. "I care about grubs and bugs too. But I also care about my friends and the Pride and the leaves and the st—"

"Enough!" snapped Timon. "I care about lots of things too. But I don't go around listing all of them unless somebody asks me."

"But you *did* ask me!" said Pumbaa.

"Stop arguing!" yelled Kopa. "I'll tell you what's wrong!"

CHAPTER 2

opa wiped away another tear.

"Kid, you're making me sad," said Timon. "It couldn't be all that bad."

"Yes, it could," said Kopa, taking a deep breath. "You know Afua, my best friend?"

"He's a nice kid," said Pumbaa. "A lion cub like you, right?"

"Well, he's not my best friend anymore," said Kopa. "He's a dope, and I hate him!"

"Slow down a minute," said Timon. "*Hate*'s a strong word. What did Afua do to make you hate him?"

Kopa looked down and started drawing in the dirt with his paw. Then he sniffed again.

"He's stupid, that's all," Kopa said.

"Really?" said Timon, scratching his head thoughtfully. "I don't remember that Afua was stupid last week, do you, Pumbaa?"

"Afua was pretty smart last week," Pumbaa said. "Maybe he ate something that made him sick. Sometimes when you feel sick, you act stupid for a few days."

Kopa shook his head. "That's silly! All Afua wants to do is hang around with Beba. He doesn't want to play with me anymore."

Timon started pacing back and forth. Then he stopped, holding his finger in the air.

"I remember now," he said with a big smile. "Beba is the cheetah cub. He runs all over the place."

"Right," said Kopa. "Afua thinks Beba is the fastest runner and the best climber and the highest jumper around."

"And what do you think?" asked Pumbaa.

"I think Beba is even stupider than Afua," said Kopa. "And I don't want to play with either of them anyway."

Timon and Pumbaa stared across the grassy plain. They could see the blue African hills far away. It was so quiet, the buzzing of the insects sounded like drums. Pumbaa smiled.

"This reminds me of the time I thought Timon was the meanest meerkat on the planet," he said.

"Oh, boy! I remember that," said Timon with a laugh. He grinned at Kopa. "I thought Pumbaa was the dopiest warthog that ever lived."

"I also thought Simba was just as bad," said Pumbaa.

"My father?" Kopa asked.

Timon nodded. "Nobody was talking to anybody."

Kopa's mouth dropped open. "You

mean all three of you guys used to hate one another?"

"*Hate* doesn't even come close," Pumbaa chuckled. "Timon and I didn't talk to each other for days!"

"And neither of us would talk to Simba," said Pumbaa. "And Simba wouldn't talk to us either."

"Right," said Timon. "When I saw Pumbaa or your dad coming, I wanted to hide."

"That's terrible," said Kopa. "What happened that made you guys so mad?"

"It wasn't our fault," said Pumbaa.

"But we didn't know that," said Timon.

"We didn't do anything wrong," Pumbaa said.

"Yeah, but who knew?" Timon shrugged.

"Slow down," said Kopa. "Somebody must have done something. Best friends never hate each other." He stopped and thought for a moment. Then he said quietly, "They only do that if one of them does something really, really bad."

"You mean something really bad like what Afua is doing to you?" asked Pumbaa.

"Right," said Kopa. "I didn't do anything to Afua. He's the one being stupid, not me!"

"Are you sure Afua is being stupid?" asked Pumbaa. "It sounds to me as though you're jealous of Beba."

"I am not jealous," said Kopa. "And you guys don't know anything!" He got up. "I'm leaving!" he said.

"I was jealous," Pumbaa said softly.

Kopa stopped. "Jealous? You?"

"I was jealous too," said Timon.

"Of who?" asked Kopa, scowling.

"It was because of that snake, Joka," said Pumbaa.

"He was a big snake," said Timon. "A python." He shivered. "Just thinking about Joka makes me feel creepy."

"Yup," said Pumbaa. "A sneaky

python tried to break up our friendship."

"And it almost worked too," said Timon.

"Now, sit down and listen," said Pumbaa. "We're going to tell you what happened."

Kopa sat down under the tree.

"Have a grub," said Timon. Kopa took the grub and chewed.

"Simba had been living with us for a few months," Pumbaa began.

"We were the best friends there ever were," said Timon. Pumbaa nodded and gave Kopa another grub.

"One day, I was alone in the jungle," said Timon, "fooling around, singing a song, doing a dance, playing a little hide-and-seek with the grubs."

CHAPTER

3

Timon heard a rustling in the leaves. He stopped dancing and cocked his head. The rustling stopped. Timon shrugged and began singing.

"Where, oh, where has my little grub gone? Oh, where, oh, where can it be?" Timon lifted a log.

He heard the rustling again.

But this time, he also heard a hissing.

"Rustling. Hmmmm," Timon said to himself. "And hissing. At the same time. Not a good sign."

The rustling and hissing stopped. Timon went back to the log. He lifted one end and shot his hand under it.

"Ah-hah! Gotcha!" He snatched up a grub and popped it in his mouth. "Oooh, goody. One of the minty ones!"

Timon lifted another log and grabbed a fat beetle. The rustling started again. He snapped his head around. Slithering through the grass was Joka, the biggest python he'd ever seen.

Joka's long, forked tongue was flicking in and out of his mouth. He was smiling. The smile was not a friendly smile.

I've seen some nasty smiles in my life, thought Timon, but this is the nastiest.

Still smiling the nasty smile, Joka stared into Timon's eyes.

"Who-ee!" Timon dropped the beetle. "I'm outta here."

"Not ssso fassst," Joka hissed. "Let'sss talk about what'sss for lunch."

Timon couldn't move. All he could do was stare back at Joka. I'm, like, hypnotized, he thought. I gotta move! I gotta scram! I gotta—

But no matter how hard he tried, Timon couldn't budge. All that moved were his teeth—and they were chattering with fright.

Joka lifted his head. His eyes were so close to Timon's face that they looked as big as plates. Joka coiled around him, and Timon felt the python's dry, smooth skin. Joka started to squeeze, his mouth wide open.

Timon heard snarling. It was Simba. He came flying over the log. He raked his claws across Joka's head. Joka's hold loosened. Timon fell to the ground. Simba knocked Timon out of the way. Then he turned to face Joka.

"Get lost!" Simba snarled. "Get away from here! And never come back!" He gave a mighty roar.

Joka lay on the ground near Simba's feet. He glared at Simba and hissed.

"Did I sssteal your meerkat sssnack?" Joka raised his head. "Findersss, keep-ersss, losersss, weepersss!"

Joka lunged toward Simba. Simba dodged. Once more, Simba's claws raked Joka's head. Then Simba leaped straight up. He came down with all four paws and pinned Joka. But Joka twisted out of Simba's grip. With an angry hiss, Joka slithered off into the grass. Timon's eyes rolled up, and he fell over in a dead faint.

"Hey! Timon! Get up!" yelled Simba, nudging him with his nose. "Are you okay? Wake up, please!"

"What happened?" asked Pumbaa, dashing into the clearing. "What's wrong with Timon?"

"Oh, man!" Simba panted. "I got here just in time! Some snake was about to eat him! Is he going to be okay?"

"Timon, ol' buddy!" said Pumbaa, pushing Timon's foot with his snout. "Speak to me! Speak to me! Don't die!"

Timon blinked, then sat up. He started patting himself all over.

"I'm alive, right?" he asked, looking a little cross-eyed. "I'm not dead or anything like that, am I?"

"No, you're right here with us," said Simba. "You had a close call. That snake almost had you for lunch!"

"Omigosh!" said Timon. "That makes me feel sick to my tummy. Eee-uuuw! Yech! What a disgusting thought!"

"You'd better not go off alone like that again," said Pumbaa. He looked around. "That snake might come back. You're my best friend! What would I do if anything happened to you?"

"Even more important, what would I do if anything happened to me?" said Timon, giving himself a shake.

"Okay, here's the plan," said Simba. "If Joka comes back for his snack, he'll have to fight all three of us. We'll stick together day and night."

"Good thinking," said Pumbaa. "That snake in the grass will never get Timon alone—ever!"

CHAPTER

While the three friends were talking, Joka was hanging from a branch over their heads. He heard everything they said.

"Sssooo, that'sss what I mussst do," Joka whispered. "I mussst get the little meerkat on hisss own. That meansss I mussst get rid of hisss fat, busssybody friendsss!"

Joka coiled himself around the branch. He needed a plan, a good one.

From what they had said, Joka knew that Timon, Simba, and Pumbaa were the best of friends. And Timon was terrified. It would be hard to get him on his own.

"I'm really in the mood for sssome tasssty meerkat," Joka muttered. "There mussst be a way!"

He kept thinking until the sun went down and the moon came up. Finally, in the middle of the night, Joka stretched. He had a plan.

"Bessst friendsss are hard to sssseparate," he hissed to himself. "Ssso the way to do thisss isss to make sssure they are not bessst friendsss anymore."

First thing the next morning, Joka slithered down the tree and looked for Pumbaa. He saw Simba standing guard over Timon, who was hunting for grubs.

"Sssimply perfect," Joka hissed. He went on a bit farther and found Pumbaa staring at a banana tree, waiting for some fruit to fall.

"A sssincere good morning."

Pumbaa jumped.

"No need to get sssoo nervousss," hissed Joka, staring into Pumbaa's eyes. "I mean you no harm. It'sss been my sssad experience that warthog gives me indigessstion."

Pumbaa didn't know whether to feel glad or insulted. Still, he couldn't take his eyes off Joka. He mumbled a good-bye and tried to run, but his feet wouldn't listen to his head. Joka continued to speak softly to Pumbaa.

"I'm sssorry to sssee that the meerkat doesssn't like you. He told me that you were ssstupid and sssmelled bad. That'sss why I decided to eat him. I didn't know you were friendsss. Friendsss don't sssay thingsss like that about each other."

Pumbaa was getting dizzy. He tried to run again, but his feet still felt as if they were stuck in mud.

"Yesss. Now he hasss the lion to protect him," Joka went on. "He'sss not your friend anymore, if he ever wasss."

Joka slithered off through the grass. When he got to the edge of the clearing, he hissed softly, "You will forget that you ever talked to me."

Pumbaa stared at the grass. He was supposed to forget something, but he couldn't remember what it was.

A few minutes later, he heard Timon and Simba singing as they ambled through the jungle. Timon was rubbing his hands together.

"Yummy, yummy, yummy, I need grubs in my tummy," sang Timon. "Boy, oh, boy, am I hungry!"

"That's a good sign," said Simba. "We were worried about you."

"What were you worried about?" asked Timon. "I'm fine. After all, there's nothing like attacking a python and winning to give a guy an appetite. And have I ever got an appetite!"

"Wait a second," said Pumbaa. "I thought the *python* attacked *you*!"

"Don't be ridiculous," said Timon. "That was only after I attacked him, see."

Simba shook his head. "I think you may have hit your head when you fainted from fright," he said. "Maybe your memory got a little messed up."

"Absolutely not!" said Timon. "What happened was, I attacked him. Then he attacked me, see. I had the whole thing under control—"

"You did?" asked Simba.

"Of course," snapped Timon. "Then you came along and knocked me down. I'd have beaten that python in a minute."

"Oh, sure," said Pumbaa. He grunted.

"I'm tough," said Timon. He spun around, pretending he was boxing.

"I need a nap," said Pumbaa. He was still feeling dizzy, but he couldn't remember why. He didn't remember Joka. All he remembered was suddenly feeling sleepy.

"A nap?" said Timon. "What for?"

"Forget the nap! Let's go to the mudhole," said Simba. "We can cool off."

"I'll stay here and rest," said Pumbaa.

"Okay, okay! It's better if Simba comes with me anyway because you're so hard to wake up," grumbled Timon. "If that python came after me, you'd probably sleep through the whole thing."

Pumbaa looked hurt. He said, "I guess you won't miss me, will you?"

Simba and Timon walked to the mudhole. Joka slithered to the ground from a tree and followed them.

"So how come mud is so cool?" asked Simba.

"I dunno," said Timon. He jumped on Simba's back and looked around. "Where do you think that snake is?"

"Don't you wanna talk about science?" asked Simba.

"No," said Timon. "Could he be behind that tree?"

"What?" asked Simba.

"I'm worried," said Timon. "Are you sure you don't see that snake?"

"I'm beginning to think you only want me around as a bodyguard," said Simba.

"Don't be silly," snapped Timon.

"But you said that Pumbaa was too

hard to wake up. You only came with—"
Simba heard a rustle in the leaves.

"Help!" Timon squeaked. "That python is out there! I heard him! Save me!"

Simba whipped around, but all he saw was a swaying vine.

"I was right," Simba said. "You only want me as a bodyguard."

Timon looked around nervously. Then he grinned at Simba. "What makes you think that?"

Simba glared at him. "So why is mud cool?"

"Who cares?" said Timon, jumping off Simba's back. "Let's go!" He ran ahead but kept looking over his shoulder to be sure Simba was following him.

Simba walked slowly, growling softly.

"All according to plan," hissed Joka, smiling. "It won't be long before that friendsssship isss over."

CHAPTER 5

The next morning, Joka found Simba lying on a rock in the sun. "Hello, big and fuzzy one. I have sssome interesssting newsss. I heard Timon tell Pumbaa that he doesssn't like having you around, but he needsss you to be hisss bodyguard. Some friend!"

Simba growled, and Joka slithered away.

A little while later, Joka found Pumbaa scratching his back on a tree. "Hello, tusssked one. Did you know I heard Timon sssay he'd rather be with Sssimba than with you? It musssst be true becaussse they go everywhere together."

Pumbaa glared at Joka and trotted off.

All day long, Joka stalked the three friends. He rustled the leaves to scare Timon. This made Timon so jumpy and cranky, Pumbaa and Simba started to think it was true that Timon couldn't stand them.

Pumbaa didn't want to believe what Joka told him, but he still felt jealous of Simba. Simba kept wondering if Joka had been telling the truth, and he was jealous of Pumbaa. Timon was mad at both of them because he thought they weren't protecting him well enough. By bedtime, nobody was talking to anybody.

But a good night's sleep makes everything look better. The next day, when they were all at the mudhole, Pumbaa picked up a clot of mud and asked, "What makes mud act like mud?"

"Mud is special magic stuff that is only found in wet places," said Timon. "It's alive, kind of like bugs, but it doesn't taste good."

"I thought mud was just regular dirt that got wet," said Pumbaa.

"That's what I thought too," said Simba.

"You only think that, Pumbaa, because you don't know anything about science," said Timon. "It's a good thing you have me to tell you how things work. You'd never figure anything out on your own."

"That's not true!" said Pumbaa. "I'm not dumb, you know!"

"Oh, yeah?" said Timon. "Well, you sure act dumb enough sometimes!"

"I wish you wouldn't say things like that to me," Pumbaa said. "You're not my best friend anymore!"

Pumbaa waddled off into the jungle.

"He'll be back," Timon said, yawning and stretching.

But the day wore on, and Pumbaa didn't come back. Every time Timon heard a noise in the jungle, he would jump up.

Finally, Timon got tired of waiting. "C'mon, kid," he said to Simba. "Let's go down to the waterfall."

"I'm worried about Pumbaa," said Simba. "We should be here when he gets back."

"I don't care if he comes back or not," said Timon. "He's not my best friend anymore."

"You don't mean that," said Simba.

"Maybe I do, and maybe I don't," said Timon. "But it doesn't matter. Pumbaa will come back when he's ready. So hurry up. You know I can't go anyplace unless you come with me. And I want to go to the waterfall."

"Well, I'm tired of you bossing me around," snapped Simba. "You don't really want me to be your friend. You just want me to protect you. You don't like anybody but yourself."

"That's not true! I like you a lot," said Timon. "I never said I didn't want to be your best friend. I just need you to go to the waterfall with me."

"You mean you care about me, but

you don't care about Pumbaa?" asked Simba.

"Well, I do care about Pumbaa," mumbled Timon. "It's just that he doesn't care about me anymore."

"Well, I care about Pumbaa," said Simba, "and I'm going to go find him. I miss him, and I want us all to be together!"

"Yeah, but the p-p-python—" stammered Timon.

"Yeah, but nothing," said Simba. "That python is miles away by now. I gave him a good scare."

And with that, Simba stalked off into the trees.

"Wait!" yelled Timon. "Don't leave me alone! Come back!"

Simba didn't turn around. Timon could hear him stomping through the leaves. Soon he couldn't hear anything.

"It's awful quiet around here," Timon whispered to himself. "In fact, it's so quiet, it's creepy."

He walked over to one side of the clearing. Then he walked back to the other side of the clearing.

"Pumbaa?" he called out. "Simba?"

Nobody answered. He looked around to be sure. *Hissssss.* Timon jumped. But it was only the wind in the giant ferns. Maybe. Timon shivered. Simba could be wrong.

Where was that python anyway?

CHAPTER

6

Pumbaa was sitting on the bank beside the waterfall. Timon had said he was dumb. Pumbaa didn't think he was dumb. Just because he didn't know all the things Timon knew didn't mean he wasn't smart.

The more Pumbaa thought about it, the sadder he felt. After all, sometimes Timon did things that were dumb too. But Pumbaa would never pick on him because of it.

He heard a sound behind him.

"Timon!" he cried, thinking his friend had come to apologize for being so mean. He was hoping Timon would tell him he was sorry for what he'd said.

"I have sssome newsss for you." Joka was hanging from a branch, swaying back and forth. He was smiling a happy python smile.

Pumbaa stood up and pawed the ground. "Get away from me!"

"Don't worry," said Joka. "I'm not going to eat you. As I said, warthogsss are bad for my digessstion. I have a messssage from your little meerkat friend."

"No kidding?" said Pumbaa. "Why should I believe you?"

"That'sss up to you."

"What did he say?" asked Pumbaa. He wanted so to hear that Timon wanted to make up.

"Not much," said Joka. "Your little friend sssaysss he doesssn't care whether you ever come back. He sssaysss that Sssimba isss hisss bessst friend now."

Joka smiled again and slithered up into the leaves.

His head hanging, Pumbaa walked to the waterfall. It was bubbling and splashing and burbling cheerfully. Pumbaa felt very uncheery. He wanted to cry.

Maybe I should sing a song, Pumbaa thought. The trouble is, I can't think of any good ones. Timon is the one who thinks up all the good songs.

Pumbaa sat for a while, his head between his hooves. He looked at his legs. I'm covered with mud, he thought. Maybe I'll go sit under the waterfall. Then he slumped to the ground. "Nobody cares whether I'm muddy or not," he said out loud. "Why bother getting washed?"

Meanwhile, Simba had looked everywhere for Pumbaa. He had gone to all the places Pumbaa liked. He'd gone to the hollow, the tree stump grub nest, the clearing, and the swinging vine spot. He'd gone all the way to the edge of the jungle, but Pumbaa was nowhere to be found.

Simba lay down to think where else he

might search. He yawned. Nap time. He
began to climb a tree so he could stretch
out on a branch. Something soft and
shiny was already up there.

Joka!

"Get out of here!" Simba snarled.

"Why ssshould I?" hissed the python.
"I'm only here with a messsage from your
little meerkat friend."

"Oh, really?" said Simba.

"Your little friend sssaysss to tell you
that the warthog isss back," said the
python. "He alssso sssaysss to tell you
they don't want to sssee you anymore.
You're no longer their friend."

Joka smiled another happy python
smile and slithered down the tree and
into the jungle.

Simba roared at Joka. It helped a little, but he missed Timon and Pumbaa.
What would he do without them? He
wouldn't have anyone to sing songs with
or eat grubs with or splash in the
waterfall with.

He began to pace. Something Joka had said seemed odd. He didn't know what it was, but something was wrong.

Simba went over every word Joka had said.

"That's it!" he roared. "Joka said Timon told him to tell me that the warthog was back!"

Simba roared again. "Wrong! Timon would never call Pumbaa the warthog. He'd call him Pumbaa! That snake lied! Timon never gave him a message at all!"

Simba furrowed his brow. Why would Joka lie? Then he knew the horrible answer. Joka had tried to eat Timon once before. Simba and Pumbaa had vowed to protect Timon, never to leave him alone.

"Omigosh!" Simba groaned. "That python's going to eat Timon! And I helped set the trap."

CHAPTER

7

imon piled a bunch of sticks in a heap. "If that crazy python shows up, I'll throw these at him. I got an arsenal."

A parrot flew by, flapping its wings, and Timon jumped, dropping a stick.

"On the other hand," mumbled Timon, "I could hide under the pile."

Another parrot flew overhead, screeching to the first one. Timon grabbed a big stick.

"But I'd be better off up a tree," said Timon, dropping the stick.

He headed toward the biggest tree. "Oh, no!" he cried. Joka was hanging down from the lowest branch.

"Well, hello, my little meerkat lunch," said Joka. "How would you like to be sssserved? With gravy or without?"

"Ooo-whee," shrieked Timon, backing up as fast as he could, right into the mudhole.

Joka slithered down the tree and across the clearing until he was facing Timon.

Timon was afraid to look Joka in the eye. He remembered what had happened the last time.

I don't want to try that hyp-no-tizing stuff again, Timon thought. I couldn't move a muscle.

He eyed his pile of sticks.

"Get lost, you big bully," Timon yelled. "Or I'll sock you in the nose!"

Timon waved his arms wildly, but Joka came closer, a very happy python smile on his face.

Timon grabbed the biggest stick from the pile. Joka kept moving closer. "Yum,

yum," he said.

Uh-oh, Timon thought. Time to run. He ran to the right. Joka cut him off. He ran to the left. Joka cut him off again.

"Can't run," Timon said to himself. "How about a hole in the ground?"

Timon started digging. Joka kept on coming, an even happier python smile on his face. Joka coiled himself around Timon, squeezing at the same time.

"Cut it out!" wheezed Timon. "Leggo of me! I hardly even know you!"

But Joka kept smiling and squeezing. "I can't wait," he said.

Timon heard a crashing in the leaves. Pumbaa burst into the clearing.

"Drop him!" yelled Pumbaa. He charged Joka. Pumbaa tried to spear Joka on a tusk, but Joka kept twisting to put Timon in the way of Pumbaa's tusks.

"I'm afraid I'll spear you by accident," Pumbaa said to Timon.

"And I'm afraid Joka will keep squeezing until I can't breathe anymore," said

Timon, gasping for air. "Take that, you wimp!" Timon squeaked. He pulled an arm free and hit Joka on the head with his fist.

"Hee-hee-hee, you're tickling me," Joka said.

Timon heard a snarl.

"Simba!" he squeaked. Simba leaped into the clearing and landed in front of the python. He bared his teeth. "Let go of my friend now!" he snarled.

"Why ssshould I?" hissed the python.

"Because if you don't," said Pumbaa, "we will have one of the best snake-meat lunches ever served in this jungle!"

With that, Pumbaa charged Joka and pushed him back against the tree trunk. This time Pumbaa pinned Joka with his tusks so the python couldn't move.

Simba leaped and landed next to Pumbaa. With a sweep of his paw, he clawed Joka.

Hissing loudly, Joka started to uncoil. Timon fell to the ground. Panting, he dragged himself out of the way.

As soon as Timon was in the clear, Pumbaa snapped his head around and hooked Joka with a tusk.

Joka wrapped himself around Pumbaa's body. He began to squeeze. Simba opened his mouth wide and clamped it on Joka's neck.

Joka flattened, and Pumbaa fell free.

"Let'sss talk," Joka said. "I can sssee that you boysss are upsssset."

"*Upset* hardly covers it," said Pumbaa.

"Ssso, I made a little missstake," Joka whined. "Jussst let go, and I promissse not to hold a grudge. No hard feelingsss, right?"

"No hard feelings at all," said Simba. "In fact, I think we should all take a little walk, don't you?"

Pumbaa nodded, and Timon piped up: "I know a nice little ravine you'll just love!"

CHAPTER

"Gosh!" Kopa gasped. His eyes were wide open. "What happened next?"

"After that, it was a piece of cake," said Timon. "Your father carried that lying python down to the ravine and dropped him over the edge."

"Yeah," said Pumbaa. "Then Timon threw some rocks in to make sure he got the message not to come back."

"Did you guys make up then?"

"We sure did," said Pumbaa. "But not right away. My feelings were still hurt."

"He still wasn't sure Joka had been lying to him," Timon said with a chuckle.

"Simba had figured out the python was lying to him. But Pumbaa was still afraid I only wanted to be friends with Simba."

"So how did you figure out what went wrong?" Kopa asked Pumbaa.

"I knew I had to hear those words from Timon's mouth," said Pumbaa. "Just because some python said them didn't mean they were true. That's why I had come back. It was lucky I got there in time to save him."

"Yeah, I remember it to this day," said Timon. "He said even though I thought he was dumb, he didn't want our friendship to be over. But if it was really over, he had to hear me say it."

"We'd been buddies too long for me to leave forever because of rumors," said Pumbaa.

"Guys can get mad at each other, but that doesn't mean they're going to be mad at each other forever," said Timon. "I told Pumbaa I still liked him and wanted him for my friend."

"So then what happened?" asked Kopa.

"The same thing that was going on before," said Pumbaa.

"First we went swimming," said Timon. "Pumbaa still needed a bath."

"I always need a bath," said Pumbaa. "I don't like 'em, but I need 'em."

"And we ate a bunch of those fat grubs that night to celebrate," said Timon. "It was a regular feast."

"And we talked about science and friendship and trust," said Pumbaa. "Because after that python had lied to us, we learned that friendship is based on trust."

Kopa sat still for a while. Then he said, "I guess maybe I should go talk to Afua."

"That would probably be a good idea," said Timon.

"I mean, Afua may not know he's hurting my feelings when he says that Beba is better at everything than I am."

"That's true," said Pumbaa. "And

besides, what does it matter if Beba is good at some things? You're good at some other things that Beba isn't good at, I bet."

"And just because someone is better at things than you are doesn't mean they're better at being a best friend than you are," said Timon.

"That's right!" said Kopa. He looked more cheerful. "I'm going right now!"

"Going where?" asked Nala. She walked up to Kopa, but he was on his way.

"Hey, see ya, Mom!" Kopa yelled over his shoulder.

"He seems much happier than when I left him here," Nala said.

"Nothing like some deep science talk to cheer a guy up," said Timon.

"What was the problem?" asked Nala.

"Nothing the cub can't handle," said Pumbaa. "Just a little disagreement between best buddies, if you know what I mean."

Nala smiled. "I know exactly what you mean," she said. "Thanks for your help."

"Piece of cake," said Timon. "That's what friends are for, right?"

Nala gave Pumbaa and Timon each a kiss. "That's what uncles are for too."

After Nala was gone, Pumbaa sighed and rolled over on his back. "Yeah, I'd almost forgotten about that lying snake."

"Not me," said Timon. "The elephant is big, and the meerkat is small. But neither ever forgets a friend—or an enemy."

"I have to say that I have never lost my trust in you," said Pumbaa with a yawn. "In fact, I think I trust you more than I trust anyone. I even bet I trust you more than you trust me."

"Are you kidding?" snapped Timon. "I definitely trust you more than you trust me! In fact I trust you so much that—"

"Whadda you mean?" Pumbaa gasped. "How can you say that? I trust you more

than you'll ever know! In fact, it hurts my feelings to hear you say that!"

"Say what?" argued Timon. "If you think for thirty seconds that your trust is greater than mine, well, then, you have another think coming, bud! I bet—"

Pumbaa turned his back. Timon stamped his foot.

"I never thought I'd see the day when you called my trust into question," said Pumbaa with a moan.

As she strolled down the path, Nala heard the two friends arguing. She smiled and shook her head. She knew nothing could come between true friends for long.